JOHN THANATOS AND THE EGYPTIAN STONE

ADITYA SHAH

INDIA · SINGAPORE · MALAYSIA

ISBN 979-8-89026-834-1

CONTENTS

ACKNOWLEDGEMENTS

My journey from writing simple essays to a whole book has been a transitional change in my life. Although, I wasn't the only one responsible for it on my journey. I would love to thank my *masi* Namita Kothari, who enhanced my vocabulary and taught me fluent English. I also wish to thank my parents, who supported me in every way and made sure I would achieve my dreams. Their encouragement propelled me forward at every step. Thank you, Notion Press, for being the air beneath my wings. Finally, a big thanks to all my readers.

Chapter 1

JOHN THANATOS

The merciless undulating waves clashed against the *Ironclad,* a ship that transported goods for a dirt-cheap price. The moon stood out against the sky like a smudge of grease on wax paper. The dark clouds loomed over the sea like an overprotective mother over her misbehaving child, enveloping the ship in darkness. A bolt of lightning zig-zagged across the with a loud bang. Along with the oppressive orchestra, beads of rain drummed down on the deck relentlessly.

The caliginous outline of the tattered ship would just be enough for a child to get nightmares till their thirties. The sail was frayed, its ends worn out. The sigil of a skull was painted in red, now faded with dust and age.

The sail post leaned precariously to the right side, swerving the ship right and left. The deck was made of pressured pine, possibly the cheapest wood they could find.

The ship's captain Jonathan La Ciao was a scraggly man with a beard matching his personality, unkempt.

He paid minimum wages to the crew and kept every single coin they earned for him. His thick accent almost made him inaudible and required an interpreter.

From inside the ship, shouting and laughter could be heard, despite the terrible storm. The lower deck had two compartments: the storage room, where the goods were stored, and the other compartment for the crew. Some groups of people played cards in the bar, whereas others would spend months confined in a claustrophobic bunk bed. The *Ironclad* was named after a menacing Viking from the 1200s. One of the bunk-bed people (as they were called) was John Thanatos, who was much of an introvert. John's job was to clean the deck, which wasn't exactly an easy job since most of the crew were quite klutzy. Today, he got a break from his shift, and he had the storm to thank.

He had been born into a family of supposed warriors. John was quite well built but not muscular and bulky. Mops of his dark brown hair plopped onto his forehead. He had bright green eyes and a chiselled nose. He had actually got on the ship not for work but because he had been chased by the Alphaniols. The Alphaniols were a vile and violent tribe native to Eternia. His family was travelling the borders of Eternia when the Alphaniols attacked. He swore vengeance on them and wanted to make sure they would perish. No one in the crew really knew about it except for Frendrix Magel, his best friend. Frendrix Magel was a plump and petite boy, about the same age as John. Freckles dotted his fair skin. He had spiky hair that popped up every now and then. As usual, Frendrix showed up in John's bunk with a toothy smirk plastered on his face.

"Hey, Johnny. How you doing?" he asked, waiting for the same usual answer. He knew John was capable of something neither of them knew yet. John was about to answer when a burly man in a brown cloak entered the bunks.

He shouted in a gruff voice, "Oy, crew! Captain wants you all in the bar now." The crew stumbled out of their beds and headed for the bar. John and Frendrix stood up and joined the serpentine queue leading to the bar.

Chapter 2

THE NEWS

The sailors assembled in the bar. Captain La Ciao stood up on a table. He stroked his salt and pepper beard and puffed his pipe, letting out a puff of cloud-like smoke.

"Attention, all crew," he boomed in his thick, Italian accent, "I have special news from the Dynasty of Warriors."

Murmurs rippled through the crowd. The *Ironclad* had only been used for transporting goods for poor merchants, unlike the deep-pocketed Dynasty of Warriors. Of course, the Dynasty weren't merchants. They were vast organizations of Japanese ninjas who were like superheroes without capes. They were quite mysterious. No one knew their leader, but they had branches all around the world. John looked up to them. They tried to save his parents from the jaws of death, but a skilled Alphaniol plunged at them with a kunai tactical knife and slit their throats. Anger boiled inside John every time he pictured their death. He wasn't there, but he was sent a letter from the Dynasty. John didn't know whether to grieve or burn with anger, but one thing was for sure, he wanted VENGEANCE.

John's thoughts were interrupted by Captain La Ciao.

"The Dynasty is paying us a hefty amount of coins to transport a sacred stone from Egypt. Since it's quite valuable, my right-hand Baldur will guard it. Don't try anything funny. My friend has a unique way of dealing with crooks."

Having said that, a hefty man, at least 6 feet, barged into the room. His bushy moustache covered his lips and nostrils. An axe slung over his brawny back. The captain introduced him as Baldur Blackbeard.

Even at midnight, John lay awake staring at the infinite blanket of stars above him. There was a whole world out there. Little did John know, he would be facing it sooner than it seemed.

Chapter 3

THE PLAN

John yawned as arrows of golden daylight filled the bunks. Another boring, humdrum day on the ship. He knocked on Frendrix's bunk. He opened the door and said, "Good morning." John wished him back, and they both sat in his bunk. John was in deep thought.

"Hey Frendrix, ever think that we could steal the stone and make some easy money? I mean, it would help to get off this rust bucket when it docks in England."

Frendrix was hesitant. "Is stealing really gonna help? I mean, we could just work for it," he replied.

"We would take our entire lives to even save up to leave the ship, let alone start an organization," John said.

"You do have a point," said Frendrix, "But even if we decide to heist it, how are we gonna get past Baldur? He could snap us like a twig. And even *you* can't fight him."

John thought for a bit and asked, "What if I took care of him? Could you pick the lock?"

"You got it."

Frendrix was an expert at picking locks and opening locked doors. That would be pretty useful.

Frendrix wondered if John would be able to fight Baldur single-handedly. He heard Baldur was an Alphaniol before he worked on the ship. What if he was going to hurt John? The heist wasn't worth it, was it?

John panted and gasped for air. He had been doing push-ups for the past two hours. Sweat trickled down his body. He had to train for this. He knelt down on his bag and removed a kunai. It gleamed in the sunlight, its blade as sharp as a lion's tooth. Leather was wound around it with a ring-like structure where his finger passed through. It was the only thing his parents had given him after their death.

The days passed as fast as lightning until the next day arrived.

The heist had begun.

Chapter 4

THE HEIST

At twelve o'clock on the dot, John and Frendrix snuck out into the room where the sacred stone was stored. Sure enough, Baldur stood there, the same old grim look on his face. John took a deep breath and took out his kunai. Frendrix was sweating, even on a cold, harsh night like this one. John felt the adrenaline pumping in him. He crouched around a few boxes, staying on his toes. Even the slightest sound would alert the brute. They didn't have a physical advantage, so their only shot would be the element of surprise. They had to take down Baldur first; he was circling the stone like a vulture over its prey. To take him down, John had to move in closer to him. He ducked as Baldur suddenly swerved in his direction. Was he spotted? His hands were sweatier now. But Baldur didn't move. He snuck up behind him. It was now or never.

John leapt onto Baldur and slit his stomach. Blood sprayed onto his face, but he barely flinched. However, he was surprised.

"You little brats, you'll pay for that!" he growled in a loud voice.

He hook-punched John with his meaty arms, sending him crashing through some wooden crates. John winced in pain and spat a blob of spit and blood. Luckily, Frendrix had already started picking the lock. John stood up.

"Come on, meathead," he said daringly.

John sprinted forward, accelerated with adrenaline, and went for another stab. He didn't want to kill him, but he needed the stone if he wanted his vengeance. But Baldur was quick on his feet and swerved to the left and counter-attacked by jabbing John in the neck, sending him crumpling to the floor like a piece of useless paper. John's body begged him to surrender, but he was determined. All he had to do was distract Baldur until Frendrix got the stone. It couldn't be that hard, could it? John wished he could take those words back as Baldur growled and whirled his axe into the air, missing John by a hair and instead digging his axe into the floorboards. John took advantage and stabbed the knife into Baldur's hand and landed a hard kick on his chest, sending him staggering back. In return, Baldur plunged at John, forcing him to the floor. He punched John in the face until blood frothed out of his mouth. Just one more punch, and it would be game over for John. Frendrix had gotten his hands on the stone and was now making his way to help John. He landed a weak but efficient kick on Baldur, giving John a chance to get back up on his feet. He swept the blood off his face with his sleeve. He held his kunai in defence and gritted his teeth. Baldur was stuck between the duo. Frendrix sprinted for another hit, but Baldur foolishly counter-attacked, giving John the opportunity to attack from behind. He put all his power into every inch of his body to land a mighty stab on Baldur's neck and a sharp blow on his spine, immobilizing him. John threw his lifeless body into the ocean for its violent waves to devour.

John and Frendrix admired the beautiful stone. Even in the dim light, it gleamed stunningly, and Egyptian hieroglyphs were carved on its purple surface. John put the stone in his pocket, and they bolted back to their bunks.

John looked at his bloody kunai and felt bad for killing Baldur. He didn't deserve this after all. John shook the thought off and went to bed.

The next morning, there was a meeting again, of course. It was regarding the stone. John and Frendrix pretended to be unaware until officially declared to arouse the least suspicion. The stone was still in his pocket when he noticed that everyone's bunks were being inspected. John panicked. They would check his pockets, too, and then, it would be the end of him and Frendrix. He gulped. They had to escape this ship soon, or it was a 'Goodbye cruel world' for them. He quickly put the stone under his tongue.

The supervisor arrived at their bunk. He checked everything, leaving no stone unturned.

He checked the bags, the pockets and even the cupboards. Finally, he turned to John and asked, "Why are you so quiet, huh? That's suspicious. You wouldn't happen to know where the stone is, would you?"

John remained silent.

"What happened? Cat got your tongue?"

Frendrix stuttered, "Uhm, uh, h-he. He lost his voice."

John nodded vigorously in approval.

The supervisor inquisitively squinted at John and finally left.

“That was close,” Frendrix said.

“Way too close,” John replied.

They headed to the bar and chugged down a mug of coffee. John knew that they would keep checking the bunks, and it wouldn’t be safe for either of them.

Chapter 5

THE ESCAPE

Another day had passed after the great heist, and the fragile string that connected them to life was on the verge of snapping. Checking became more regular and thorough. After hours of waiting, John Thanatos finally found their next stop, England. That night, they were going to stop by England to drop off a small crate, so they started packing their belongings. John kept his kunai in his pocket. They met in his bunk and discussed the plan. They would be on the deck a mile away from the dock. They would then jump into the sea around 200 metres away from land. Simple, yet so deadly.

The rest of the day passed like a quick bang of lightning. In the distance, Frendrix spotted land, England. They got on deck, but there was a problem. Guards were crawling everywhere. They were armed to the teeth with bows and arrows. John and Frendrix pretended to sweep the deck. On John's signal, they would leap into the waters. John threw the broom on the closest guard's head and shoved him to the ground. The rest circled around him. Perfect. Frendrix leapt off the deck as planned. John removed his kunai. The hulking brutes attacked at once, but John's knife slashed through their armoured chests, and he plunged into the murky waters. He could feel arrows whizzing past him. His chest was tight. If he went to the surface, he would be shot to death. He kept a steady mind and swam towards shore. Only for a split second, he popped to the surface for a breath and dove back in. He could see Frendrix signalling him to swim faster. Finally, he reached the shore, wheezing for breath. But there was no time to waste. The guards were already gaining on them. They ran through the narrow, elegant streets, dodging horse carts and confused citizens. John never knew his first time in the real world would be so petrifying, yet he admired the quaint Victorian architecture. Suddenly, a guard stopped them. John knew he had to kill him, or else he would die too. He pulled out his kunai and held it menacingly. No, he wouldn't do it. He wasn't going to kill another person in cold blood. He just pushed the guard hard and whizzed through the lanes. In the distance, he saw a thick and dense forest behind a hedge. Would he make the jump? It was a leap of faith. He let himself lift his body high enough to jump over the wall. They made it once again, barely alive, though. Frendrix was gasping and panting for breath. They sat amongst thick foliage where they wouldn't be spotted. Sweat trickled down their cheeks. After regaining their breath, they made their way deeper into the forest. Bushes lined a muddy path amongst the thick shadowy trees. The leaves were wet with dew as moonlight passed through the canopy of trees. The captain would've docked for a week or so until they found the stone. He admired the stone, a dark purple gemstone. He would make a whole lot of money with it, although a part of him wanted to decipher the hieroglyphs. John shuffled over to Frendrix, his legs still sore from running. Search parties would be there by dawn. They had to move quickly. He thought about how they could reach Egypt to confirm the antique's value. Of course, the Egyptians would be more than happy to regain something from their land. But they needed transport, something cheap. Frendrix piped in, "We could cut a deal with a horse cart rider and give him a share of our wealth. It would take five months to reach there."

"That's not exactly a bad idea. A good one, actually, a very good one."

Chapter 6

THE FOREST

After sleeping in the woods, John thought he would never feel his back again. The sharp rock felt like they were digging into his skin. Frendrix cracked his numb joints and stifled a yawn. They sauntered deeper into the forest after freshening up. On the way, they plucked luscious berries from bushes pregnant with fruit. Sunlight passed through the canopy of leaves. In the distance, they saw majestic mountains, painted in streaks of white and blue, standing against the golden sun. As they trekked further, John suddenly knew something was fishy. It had been hours, and they did not come across a single guard. He kept his eyes glued on the bushes and hedges in case of a surprise attack. He alerted Frendrix about his suspicions.

Frendrix coolly replied, "Maybe they are just afraid to attack us. I mean, we did kind of beat them up. And if they do come, it's like asking for a beating. Relax, John."

"Just keep an eye out," John said firmly.

The sun's heat made their skin moist with sweat. Noon was near, and not a single sign of the soldiers. Their legs were aching now. John trudged with slow, heavy steps. In the distance, they saw a hut. Frendrix said, "We could go in there and ask for food. I mean, it wouldn't be a bad idea after all. We *need* food."

John didn't reply. He made his way towards the hut with quicker steps now. They knocked on the heavy oak door. The hut was quaint and small. The roof was thatched with hay, and the walls were made of toughened rosewood. The windows were designed as arches with tinted glass. Frendrix knocked again, this time louder. The door was opened by an old woman. She had wrinkles all over her skin. She had small eyes and a hollow socket. She had snowy white hair, quite petite in height, though.

"Welcome, visitors." She croaked. She led them into the kitchen and put on some tea in the kettle. She asked them where they came from. John gulped, saying, "Uh, we come from the East."

"Well, I don't get many visitors in the woods these days."

Frendrix enquired, "Why do you live here, away from the towns?"

The woman didn't reply, but instead, she drew apart her curtains. John and Frendrix saw a new version of life apart from bloodshed and violence and, of course, rat-infested ships. Undulating rolling hills sprinkled the landscape. Trees dotted the picturesque scenery. Birds warbled as if they were confabulating with each other. The calm wind's waltz rustled the leaves, heavy with dew.

"Whoa, lady, you are lucky," Frendrix exclaimed.

She smiled, showing her broken, crooked teeth. They thanked the woman heartily for the herbal tea she had made for them.

She bid goodbye, but before that, she gifted them two horses, jet black. The woman said, "Thanatos once helped me, and now, it is time to repay my debt."

What!!! How had she known about his family?! Before he could ask her more about them, Frendrix tugged him and led him to the horses.

Chapter 7

THE FINALE

John mounted his horse and gripped the leather reins. Frendrix did the same. They galloped at top speed. The wind made their hair stick up straight. John had never ridden a horse before. He lurched back and forth. After three hours or so, they could see a vast meadow, probably a farm. But it was surrounded by high wooden walls. They couldn't go further. Their horses grazed while they figured out how to pass the gate. Suddenly, John noticed guards. They were everywhere, scouring the fields for them. They would be caught soon. Jack and Frendrix lay down amongst the long grass. It was an ambush. John whispered, "We can't escape. We only have one choice." Frendrix grinned.

They emerged from the grass stealthily and plunged at the guards. John twirled and kicked a guard in the face sending him crashing to the ground. He got up and knocked John down with a punch. John leapt up and forward and slit the guard's throat with his kunai. Another guard caught hold of John and started strangling him, but he was put down with a heavy blow by Frendrix.

"You're welcome," Frendrix smirked. Three more guards attacked. This time, they had swords. One of them swung their sword, but John ducked and punched him straight in the stomach. Before he could regain his energy, he felt a sharp twinge of pain. He had been stabbed. The pain was now gruelling. Another guard took advantage of this and kicked John in the face. Blood trickled down his nose and mouth. Frendrix was knocked unconscious. John grated his teeth and punched his enemy, sending him hurling through the air. He felt the wind of the sword barely an inch away from his neck. John took out his kunai and flung it at the guard's chest. The guard spluttered cold red blood onto the grass. The last one ran away. John shook Frendrix. He didn't get up. An arrow whizzed past John. His senses were alerted, and he stood up. A surly and buff man stood in front of him. John cursed him and bolted towards him. The man punched John hard in the jaw. A crack broke the silence. John's jaw was broken, and blood spilt out of his mouth. Another blow, a kick, landed on his chest. It felt as if his lungs were on fire. He punched the man back, but he didn't even blink. The next thing John knew, he was being strangled on the ground. He winced as he got up. He tried to slit the man's throat, but the man grabbed the kunai and stabbed John instead. Pain shot up through his body. He landed a weak punch, only to be kicked in the chest. It was goodbye for John now. He felt the gemstone in his hand. The moment his fingers touched the stone, all his wounds healed almost magically. A sudden burst of energy surged through his veins. He leapt onto the man and smashed the stone on his chest. Blood sprayed onto the stone. The stone was something magical. John's fists were glowing purple. There was so much power in him. He punched the man, sending him hurling towards the wall, smashing it to pieces. He growled and jumped onto John, but John punched him harder, cracking his ribs. He sprinted towards the man's body and crushed it with another mighty blow. The stone had saved him. It had actually saved him. He rushed towards Frendrix, his heart palpitating. He gripped the stone in his scarred hand and held it on Frendrix's chest. The stone hummed, but nothing happened. John took a deep breath and tried again, this time harder. His eyes were stinging as he held back the tears brimming his eyes. Had the stone reached its limit?

John burst out crying. He lost something more precious than even a hundred shimmering pieces of sapphire. All because of a stupid stone. He howled and clenched the stone harder than ever and tried one final time, his last hope. The stone made an eerie humming sound before stopping abruptly. It was the end. He turned around to walk away, each sight of his best friend brimming his heart with remorse. The ravens eulogized over his best friend's corpse.

A voice suddenly shouted, "Hey, you gonna leave me here, mate?"

John turned, his eyes hopeful, and he saw the one thing that couldn't make him any happier. His happiness exceeded words, and he tightly wrapped his arms around his friend.

"You wanna kill me again?" Frendrix laughed. "You're suffocating me."

John wiped the tears off his face and retorted, "You couldn't wake up earlier!"

Frendrix just gave back a cheeky smile. He hadn't seen him smile for donkey's years.

John was too tired to grin and collapsed on the ground. His eyes gazed at the crimson sky, watching the magnificent sun's descent. His eyes were heavy, and before he knew it, they were deep in slumber.

What the duo didn't know was that with the great power they held, more maniacs would be after them.

ABOUT THE AUTHOR

Aditya Shah lives in Mumbai, India, with his parents.

From a young age, he has been a voracious reader and dreamt of having his book published.

Aditya published his first book at the young age of eleven, chasing his dreams till they became a reality.

His hobbies include playing soccer and reading novels, and of course, playing battle royale video games. He adores animals and hopes to own a Husky one day.

Aditya is currently working on the sequel of this series, and it will be out sooner than you think!

www.ingramcontent.com/pod-product-compliance
Lightning Source LLC
La Vergne TN
LVHW091243150826
845673LV00003B/1263

* 9 7 9 8 8 9 0 2 6 8 3 4 1 *